Dear Parents:

Congratulations! Your child is taking the first steps on an exciting journey. The destination? Independent reading!

STEP INTO READING® will help your child get there. The program offers five steps to reading success. Each step includes fun stories and colorful art or photographs. In addition to original fiction and books with favorite characters, there are Step into Reading Non-Fiction Readers, Phonics Readers and Boxed Sets, Sticker Readers, and Comic Readers—a complete literacy program with something to interest every child.

P9-DZP-176

Learning to Read, Step by Step!

Ready to Read   Preschool–Kindergarten
• big type and easy words • rhyme and rhythm • picture clues
For children who know the alphabet and are eager to begin reading.

Reading with Help   Preschool–Grade 1
• basic vocabulary • short sentences • simple stories
For children who recognize familiar words and sound out new words with help.

Reading on Your Own   Grades 1–3
• engaging characters • easy-to-follow plots • popular topics
For children who are ready to read on their own.

Reading Paragraphs   Grades 2–3
• challenging vocabulary • short paragraphs • exciting stories
For newly independent readers who read simple sentences with confidence.

Ready for Chapters   Grades 2–4
• chapters • longer paragraphs • full-color art
For children who want to take the plunge into chapter books but still like colorful pictures.

STEP INTO READING® is designed to give every child a successful reading experience. The grade levels are only guides; children will progress through the steps at their own speed, developing confidence in their reading.

Remember, a lifetime love of reading starts with a single step!

To Ruby, who will always be my first princess
—J.L.

Step into Reading, Random House, and the Random House colophon are registered trademarks of Penguin Random House LLC.

Visit us on the Web!
StepIntoReading.com
randomhousekids.com

Educators and librarians, for a variety of teaching tools, visit us at RHTeachersLibrarians.com

ISBN 978-0-7364-3666-3 (trade) — ISBN 978-0-7364-8192-2 (lib. bdg.)
ISBN 978-0-7364-3667-0 (ebook)

Printed in the United States of America   10 9 8 7 6 5 4 3 2

DISNEY
PRINCESS

What Is a Princess?

by Jennifer Liberts

illustrated by Atelier Philippe Harchy

Random House 🏠 New York

What is a princess?

A princess is kind.

Snow White gives

Grumpy a big kiss.

A princess is smart.
Belle reads
lots of books.

A princess is caring.
Belle helps the Beast
when he is hurt.

What is a princess?

A princess is brave.

Jasmine stands up

to the evil Jafar.

A princess is
ready for fun.
Jasmine flies
through the sky.

A princess
loves to explore.

Ariel finds
a sunken ship.

A princess is
a dreamer.

Ariel wishes

to go on land.

What is a princess?

A princess is polite.

"Thank you,"
says Briar Rose.

A princess loves

to sing and dance.

And a princess always lives happily ever after!